Ms. Schnickle's
Class

Tom-Tom

Teddy

Polly

Lulu

Dolly

Eddie

Joan

For Margot and Lila,
whose school days will be starting soon!
Love, Iza

RUFUS AND FRIENDS
SCHOOL DAYS

Traditional poems
extended and illustrated by
Iza Trapani

ini Charlesbridge

RUFUS AND FRIENDS
SCHOOL DAYS

My books are packed. My tummy's fed.

I'm ready for the day ahead.

It's raining out, but that's okay.

The bus is here. I'm on my way.

My teacher and my friends are great.

We're off to school, and I can't wait!

Why don't you hop aboard this bus

And spend a day in school with us?

SCHOOL BUS

The Ants Go Marching

The ants go marching one by one,
Hurrah, hurrah!
The ants go marching one by one,
Hurrah, hurrah!
The ants go marching one by one,
The little one stops to suck his thumb,
And they all go marching down
To the ground
To get out
Of the rain.
Boom! Boom! Boom! Boom!

6

Like ants they're marching through the hall,
Heigh-ho, heigh-ho!
In single file along the wall,
Heigh-ho, heigh-ho!
They march in step, in perfect rows,
The little one stops to pick her nose,
And they all go marching fast
To their class
To have fun
One by one!
Two! Three! Four! Five!

Come Hither, Little Puppy Dog

Come hither, little puppy dog.
I'll give you a new collar
If you will learn to read your book
And be a clever scholar.

Come over, little waggly pups.
Let's have our morning greeting.
We'll talk about our day ahead,
And then we'll start off reading.

We'll also write and draw and sing
And learn some things worth knowing.
It's going to be a busy day,
So puppies, let's get going!

There's a Neat Little Clock

There's a neat little clock,
In the schoolroom it stands,
And it points to the time
With its two little hands.

And may we, like the clock,
Keep a face clean and bright,
With hands ever ready
To do what is right.

ABC
DEFG
HIJK
LMNO
PQRS
TUVW
XYZ

Red + Yellow = Orange
Yellow + Blue = Green
Blue + Red = Purple

Paw Paint

And we do what we can
With our two little hands,
But our projects don't always
Turn out as we planned.

We are ready to work.
Our spirits are keen.
Our faces are bright,
But they're not always clean.

Though we try very hard,
Still it isn't so rare
To find paint on our noses
Or glue in our hair.

11

When at last we are done,
We can stand proud and tall,
And our work is displayed
On the wall in the hall.

One Thing at a Time

One thing at a time,
And that done well,
Is a very good rule,
As many can tell.

One word at a time,
And soon you'll know
So many new words.
You'll read like a pro!

Ask
By
Could
Did
Every
From
Good
Has
Into
Just
Know
Like
May

New
Over
Please
Quick
Round
Some
Take
Under
Very
What
X-ray
Yes
Zoo

There Was a Little Girl

There was a little girl
Who had a little curl
Right in the middle of her forehead.
When she was good,
She was very, very good,
But when she was bad, she was horrid.

The horrid little girl,
Who liked to twirl her curl,
Growled with a scowl as she pouted.
Oh, she was sour.
How she howled for an hour!
But then she forgot all about it.

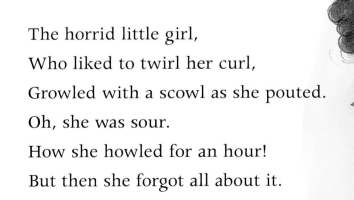

1 Sing, 1 Sing

I sing, I sing,

From morn till night.

From cares I'm free, and my heart is light.

I read, I read,
Each book in sight.
As you can see, I'm very bright.

I write, I write,
With all my might.
It's hard for me, but I write right.

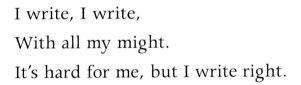

A Diller, a Dollar

A diller, a dollar,

A ten o'clock scholar.

What makes you come so soon?

You used to come at ten o'clock,

But now you come at noon.

A dozer, a drowser,
A slow-rousing bowser,
You sleep just like a rock.
School starts at eight, but you're not late.
It's only twelve o'clock!

SHAPES

Piping Hot! Smoking Hot!

Piping hot!
Smoking hot!
What I've got, you have not.
Hot gray peas, hot, hot, hot,
Hot gray peas, hot.

Tough to chew!
Thick as glue!
Just one scoop. Please, not two!
Chewy stew, chew, chew, chew,
Gluey goo, eeeeew!

Intery, Mintery, Cutery Corn

Intery, mintery, cutery corn,
Apple seed and briar thorn.
Wire, briar, limber lock,
Five geese in a flock.
Sit and sing by a spring.
O-U-T and in again.

Buttery, puttery, chicory, rue,
Honey cake and tea for two.
Tansy, pansy, purple chive,
Five bees in a hive.
Down below flowers grow.
O-U-T and out they go!

Here I Am, Little Jumping Joan

Here I am, little jumping Joan.
When nobody's with me, I'm always alone.

When nobody's with me, I'll find a nice spot
And sit down to read, for I love books a lot.

Here I am, little jumping Joan.
When I have a book, I'm never alone.

On the chalkboard:

1 one
2 two
3 three
4 four
5 five
6 six
7 seven
8 eight
9 nine
10 ten

$$9 + 1 = 10$$
$$5 - 1 = 4$$
$$3 + ...$$
$$4 + 5 = 9$$
$$8 - 2$$

Math Words: add plus
subtract minus

One, Two, Buckle My Shoe

One, two, buckle my shoe.
Three, four, shut the door.
Five, six, pick up sticks.
Seven, eight, lay them straight.
Nine, ten, a big fat hen.

One, two, why don't you,
Three, four, count some more?
Five, six, arithmetic,
Seven, eight, is really great!
Nine, ten, now back again.

24

Ten, nine, you're doing fine!
Eight, seven, it's math heaven!
Six, five, can you survive,
Four, three, this counting spree?
Two, one. Phew! You're done!

Tom, Tom, the Piper's Son

Tom, Tom, the piper's son.
He learned to play when he was young.
He with his pipe made such a noise
That he pleased all the girls and boys.

Toot! Toot! He piped his flute.
He was a hoot, the cute galoot.
All of the kids began to cheer
When Tom-Tom tooted loud and clear!

Polly, Dolly, Kate, and Molly

Polly, Dolly, Kate, and Molly,

All are filled with pride and folly.

Polly tattles, Dolly wriggles,

Katy rattles, Molly giggles.

Whoever knew such constant rattling,

Wriggling, giggling, noise, and tattling?

Eddie, Freddie, Mops, and Teddy,
All are feeling rough and ready.
Eddie bumbles, Freddie pounces,
Mopsy tumbles, Teddy bounces.
Who can stand such constant tumbling,
Pouncing, bouncing, buzz, and bumbling?

If You're Happy and You Know It, Clap Your Hands

If you're happy and you know it, clap your hands.

If you're happy and you know it, clap your hands.

If you're happy and you know it,

Then your face will surely show it.

If you're happy and you know it, clap your hands.

If you're learning and you know it, nod your head.

Do you pay attention to what's being said?

There is always something new

You can learn and you can do.

If you're learning and you know it, nod your head.

If you're curious and you know it, wink your eye.

Do you want to know what, where, when, how, and why?

Go ahead and raise your hand.

Ask until you understand.

If you're curious and you know it, wink your eye.

If you love school and you know it, shout hurray!

Do you have a lot of fun in school each day?

With the teacher as your guide,

And your good friends by your side,

If you love school and you know it, shout hurray!

Wink your eye!

Nod your head!

Clap your hands!

We all enjoyed your company,
But now we're off. The clock says three.
We have some homework still to do,
And here's a fun-filled quiz for you!

1. Pages 8–9: Find these hidden words: chalk, crayon, marker, pen, and pencil. What do these objects have in common?

2. Pages 10–11: Find a red triangle, a green circle, a blue rectangle, and a yellow square.

3. Pages 18–19: Find two clocks and three watches. What time is it on each?

4. Pages 22–23: Find these hidden words: fun, play, skip, swing, and throw. Practice writing them down.

5. Pages 24–25: Five purple numbers (1, 2, 3, 4, 5) are hidden. Find them and write them down, then add them all up.

6. Pages 26–27: Can you find and name all ten instruments?

7. Pages 28–29: Find the hidden red letters R, E, A, D, I, N, and G. Then think of some words that begin with each of these letters and write them down!

Quiz Answers:

1. You can write or draw with them.

3. The clock in the cubby reads 8:00, the clock on the wall reads 12:00, the watch on Ms. Schnickle's dress reads 10:00, Mr. Boss's watch reads 12:00, and the watch in the bookshelf reads 3:15.

5. $1 + 2 + 3 + 4 + 5 = 15$

6. maracas, cymbals, kazoo, tambourine, guitar, drum, harmonica, xylophone, bongo, recorder

34

Dear Friends,

I started first grade in America in the fall of 1961, after moving from my birth country, Poland. I showed up to class with a leather backpack and a pair of slippers. As is the custom for Polish schoolchildren, I put on the slippers before taking my seat. All eyes turned toward me, followed by an outburst of giggles. I was mortified. Although I knew how to read and write in Polish, I had only memorized a handful of English words, so I had no idea what anyone was saying or why they were laughing at me.

At lunchtime my classmates surrounded me, and I realized that their faces were genuinely inquisitive and friendly. They told me their names and offered me snacks from their lunch boxes. We communicated with simple gestures, exchanging English and Polish words and enjoying the sounds of them. All at once I became part of a community. It felt good.

English came to me quickly, with the help of my teachers, friends, and a Mother Goose treasury that I read most days after school. The fun sounds facilitated my learning and instilled in me a lasting love of poetry and language.

The rhymes in this book are all traditional, and I have extended them with a stanza or more of my own words. I wanted to show Rufus and his pals as part of a larger community, so the school theme was a natural choice. Our school days are a vital time of growth and discovery. I look back on mine fondly. Enjoy!

Warm wishes,

Iza

Text and illustrations copyright © 2010 by Iza Trapani
All rights reserved, including the right of reproduction in whole or in part in any form.
Charlesbridge and colophon are registered trademarks of Charlesbridge Publishing, Inc.

The first verse of "There Was a Little Girl" was written by Henry Wadsworth Longfellow.
The first verse of "If You're Happy and You Know It, Clap Your Hands" is usually credited to Alfred B. Smith.
The remaining poems are traditional, and all have been extended by the author.

Published by Charlesbridge
85 Main Street
Watertown, MA 02472
(617) 926-0329
www.charlesbridge.com

Illustrations done in watercolor, ink, and colored pencil
    on Fabriano 300-pound watercolor paper (soft press)
Display type and text type set in Chalk Dust, Hip Hop,
    and Apollo MT
Color separations by Chroma Graphics, Singapore
Printed and bound September 2009 in Nansha,
    Guangdong, China by Everbest Printing Company, Ltd.
    through Four Colour Imports Ltd., Louisville, Kentucky
Production supervision by Brian G. Walker
Designed by Diane M. Earley

Library of Congress Cataloging-in-Publication Data
Trapani, Iza.
    Rufus and friends : school days / extended and
illustrated by Iza Trapani.
        p. cm.
    Summary: A collection of traditional rhymes illustrated
and adapted to a school setting, with hidden objects for
the reader to find in the illustrations.
    ISBN 978-1-58089-248-3 (reinforced for library use)
    ISBN 978-1-58089-249-0 (softcover)
1. Nursery rhymes. 2. Children's poetry. [1. Nursery
rhymes. 2. Picture puzzles.] I. Title.
PZ8.3.T686Rw 2010
398.8—dc22   2009004307

Printed in China
(hc) 10 9 8 7 6 5 4 3 2 1
(sc) 10 9 8 7 6 5 4 3 2 1